The Mystery of Miss Hill's Missing Glasses!

Written by

ALISON HEPBURN

Enjoy the book!

Alison Hepburn.

For Declan, Alan, and Pamela. xxx

Published in association with Bear With Us Productions

©2021 Alison Hepburn
The right of Alison Hepburn as the author of this work has been asserted by her in accordance with the Copyright Designs and Patents Act 1988.

ISBN 978-1-3999-0079-9

Illustration by Novel Varius
Graphic Design by Luis Volkweis

justbearwithus.com

The Mystery of Miss Hill's Missing Glasses!

Written by

ALISON HEPBURN

Illustrated by

NOVEL VARIUS

BEAR WITH US

PRODUCTIONS

"Good morning, boys and girls," the children heard Miss Hill say.

Room 7 were all wondering what
they would do in school that day.

But Miss Hill looked quite different,
standing at the front of class.

What was it that had changed?
Then Callum went ahead and asked.

"The problem was, without my
glasses, I could hardly see,

So, I didn't know where my glasses
were or what was in front of me!

I'm sure I lost them just as
I approached the front school gate.

I quickly looked around,
but I didn't want to be late!"

"Now, boys and girls, I'm not too sure
of the learning we'll do today.

I really can't see properly because
my glasses have blown away!"

Then Cassie shouted out to say,
"I know what we should do!

The class can work together and help
to find your glasses for you."

Aria had a great idea
and shared it with everyone:

"We should make some posters, and
hang them up when we're done.

When everyone goes out to play,
they can all look about,

And if they find the glasses, they
can give our class a shout."

The boys and girls got started,
buzzing around like busy bees!

Writing slogans, drawing pictures,
creating posters for all to see.

They drew pictures of the glasses
and wrote messages to say:

"Can everyone look out
for Miss Hill's glasses;
they've blown away?!"

They placed the posters perfectly 'round
the school for all to see.

It was such an important job to do.
Everyone did agree.

They also asked the other children
to keep their eyes well peeled,

And look everywhere from the school gates
along to the football field.

But then playtime came and went,
and the glasses hadn't been found,

Even with the children hunting up
and down the playground.

Miss Hill's class were disappointed,
but it was time for another plan.

"We really want to help you find
your glasses if we can."

Then Conner said, "I have an idea,
I read in a detective book,

I think it will really help us to know
where we should go to look."

He asked Miss Hill if she would mind
re-enacting the event.

Then the children would see clearly,
where the glasses really went.

Miss Hill thought this was a great idea
and started to get ready.

She swiftly put her jacket on,
as did Jess, Carson and Freddie.

When everyone was sorted,
they all started to head outside.

The children were all in detective mode
with eyes and minds open wide.

When the class were all lined up, and
slowly heading towards the door,

They spotted Miss Hill's jacket
looking different from before.

Her hood was in a fankle
and was sticking up in the air.

There was something tangled
in the fabric next to Miss Hill's hair.

"Stop!" the children shouted.
"We think we've solved the mystery!"

The children had spotted the glasses
and were almost giddy with glee.

Miss Hill was looking puzzled
and her eyebrows made a frown.

The children asked Miss Hill
if she would mind kneeling down.

Then Ellie reached into the hood of Miss Hill's warm red jacket. She pulled out Miss Hill's glasses as the children made a racket.

They whooped and cheered, clapped and whistled,
and they all jumped around.
The mystery was solved;
Miss Hill's glasses
had been found!

"The wind certainty didn't blow my glasses away very far.

I'm so glad you helped me find them!

What a lovely class you are!"

After everyone settled down again, before they went for lunch,

Miss Hill told the class once more
that they were such a wonderful bunch.

They'd used lots of skills and talents,
including teamwork, English, and art.

"I'm so proud of all you've done today.
You all played a helpful part."

Sammy asked Miss Hill if sometime she thought it would be okay,

"If the wind could blow your glasses
off again another day?"

As the children left the class,
Miss Hill was wearing a great big smile.

"You never know, Sammy,
but hopefully not for a while."

Printed in Great Britain
by Amazon